Andy Pa[...]
and the whit[...]

Story by Maria Bird
Illustrated by Matvyn Wright

HODDER AND STOUGHTON
LONDON SYDNEY AUCKLAND TORONTO

Andy Pandy and Teddy have many toys. The one they love most is Looby Loo, but they are very fond of a white kitten who sleeps in a basket just the right size. All you can see is a ball of white fluff and two bright blue eyes.

The white kitten is very pretty but rather naughty, and when it does naughty things its eyes begin to look green. Sometimes by the end of the day they are as green as grass.

One day the white kitten got on the breakfast table and put its head in the milk jug. Andy Pandy lifted it out and said, 'Little cats must not jump on the table.' 'And they mustn't drink out of jugs,' said Teddy.

Andy Pandy thought the kitten was sorry it had been naughty until he saw that its eyes were turning green. The very next minute the kitten jumped out of his arms on to Teddy's head.

Teddy did look funny
with a white kitten on his
head just like a hat. Andy
Pandy laughed, but he
managed to pour out
Teddy's milk without
spilling it. But as soon as
Teddy lifted it to drink . . .

The kitten made a dash for it, slipped over Teddy's face, and down went Teddy and the kitten and the milk jug and all the milk. Andy Pandy went to pick them up but the white kitten ran out of the house as fast as it could.

The kitten stayed away all day. It didn't even come back for its dinner. Andy Pandy put it out for him, then he went out with Teddy to play. When the kitten saw them go, it crept quietly into the house.

Now although Looby Loo
was only a rag doll and
didn't talk to Andy or Teddy,
she knew how to talk to
white kittens, and she said,
'Why are you so naughty?
One day your eyes will be
so green that they will stay
green for ever and ever.'

'Pooh,' said the kitten. 'Green eyes are nice.' And before Looby Loo could say any more, it ran three times round the table, and then flew straight over to the fireplace and went up the chimney.

When the kitten didn't come home, Andy Pandy and Teddy began to wonder where it could be. They saw Looby Loo pointing to the chimney, but they didn't know she was trying to tell them where the kitten was.

They looked all over the house, under the beds, in the cupboards, in all the jampots, even in the teapot, but no white kitten. Then Andy Pandy said, 'We must go out and see if we can find it in the garden.'

But it wasn't in the garden. Andy and Teddy went along to the little wood where they played. They looked under logs and up into the trees, but all they saw were a few sleepy little birds and a field mouse.

At last they had to give up looking for the kitten. 'It's nearly dark,' Andy Pandy said. 'We must look again in the morning.' He was very sad, and a big tear rolled down his cheek.

But when they got home,
there was the white kitten
tucked up in Andy Pandy's
bed, fast asleep.

Then Andy Pandy took the
kitten very gently in his
arms to put it into its own bed.
The kitten was so tired
that it hardly moved.
It just opened its eyes for a
moment and Andy Pandy
saw that they were
bright blue.

Copyright 1954 Andy Pandy Ltd

ISBN 0 340 03067 4

First published 1954 by Brockhampton Press Ltd
(now Hodder and Stoughton Children's Books)
Reprinted 1987

Published by Hodder and Stoughton Children's Books,
a division of Hodder and Stoughton Ltd,
Mill Road, Dunton Green, Sevenoaks, Kent TN13 2YJ

Printed in Great Britain by Cambus Litho, East Kilbride